To Gordon Furry,
who has found a new home,
and to my dear dog Sara,
who has run on ahead

The artist used watercolours and pencil crayons
to create the illustrations for this book.

National Library of Canada Cataloguing in Publication Data

Muller, Robin
    Badger's new house

ISBN 0-439-98734-2

    I. Title.

PS8576.U424B32 2002   jC813'.54   C2001-902632-3
PZ7.M9184Bad 2002

5 4 3 2 1   Printed in the U.S.A.   02 03 04 05

BADGER'S NEW HOUSE

written and illustrated by

Robin Muller

North Winds Press

A Division of Scholastic Canada Ltd.

Badger lived in a cozy little house. Sometimes the door stuck. Sometimes the shutters rattled and the roof leaked. Sometimes the chimney clogged and filled the house with smoke. But Badger never seemed to mind. "Nothing's perfect," he would say.

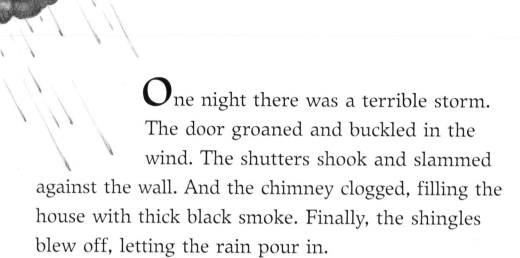

One night there was a terrible storm. The door groaned and buckled in the wind. The shutters shook and slammed against the wall. And the chimney clogged, filling the house with thick black smoke. Finally, the shingles blew off, letting the rain pour in.

The next morning when the storm had passed, Badger looked around his little home.

"This place is a mess," he said. "It needs fixing up. But I can't do it. I'm moving!"

Badger found himself an enormous new house. It had leaded windows and double doors. It had carvings and towers and polished floors. It even had a grand stone staircase at the front.

"Now this is a house!" Badger beamed and hurried home to pack.

But when he was done, his old home looked so empty and sad that he began to regret moving. Badger had an idea. He made a sign that read HANDYMAN SPECIAL—NEW OWNER NEEDED FOR OLD HOUSE.

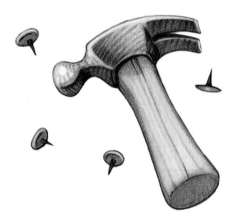

No sooner had Badger tacked it up and closed the door than there was a knock. When he opened the door, he found Grandmother Mouse holding the sign.

Badger warned her about all the repairs the house needed, but Grandmother Mouse just smiled. "Someone will fix them for me," she said.

So Badger moved into his new house, and Grandmother Mouse moved into his old one.

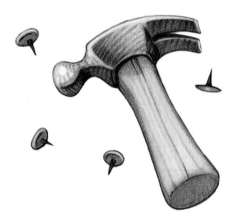

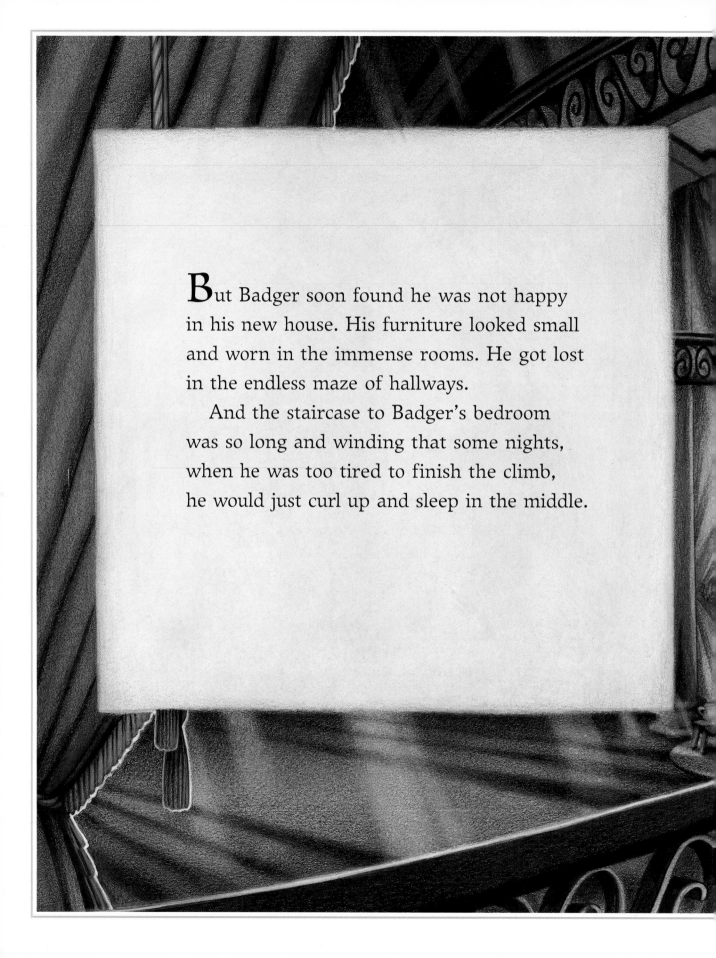

But Badger soon found he was not happy
in his new house. His furniture looked small
and worn in the immense rooms. He got lost
in the endless maze of hallways.

And the staircase to Badger's bedroom
was so long and winding that some nights,
when he was too tired to finish the climb,
he would just curl up and sleep in the middle.

One day Badger received a card from Grandmother Mouse inviting him to tea. When he arrived, his old home looked so warm and welcoming that a tear came to his eye.

"Oh, Mr. Badger," said Grandmother Mouse when she answered the door. "I want to thank you for this little house. It's perfect, just perfect."

She smiled sweetly and said, "The only thing that bothers me is the door that sticks."

Badger twisted his tie nervously. He was ashamed to admit that he'd never tried to fix anything before.

"Maybe it needs oiling," he said, mustering his courage. "Let me try." Badger picked up an oil can and began squirting the hinges. Soon the door opened smoothly.

"I fixed it!" he shouted excitedly.

They had a wonderful visit. When Badger was ready to leave, Grandmother Mouse said, "Come again tomorrow," and waved good-bye.

When he returned the next day, Grandmother Mouse was watching from the window.

"Oh, Mr. Badger," she cried. "Thank you for repairing that sticking door. Now this cozy little house is perfect, just perfect—except for the shutters that rattle." She looked at him hopefully.

"They probably need gluing," said Badger cautiously. "Let me try." With clamps, a brush, and a pot of glue, Badger repaired the broken shutters.

"I fixed them!" he exclaimed delightedly.

Again they had a wonderful visit. "Please come tomorrow," said Grandmother Mouse as she showed him to the door.

When he returned the next day, Grandmother Mouse was standing on the path.

"Oh, Mr. Badger," she cried. "Thank you for fixing that sticking door and those rattling shutters. Now this quaint little house is perfect, just perfect—except for the roof that leaks." She looked at him encouragingly.

"You just need a shingle or two," Badger replied confidently. With a hammer, nails, new shingles, and a tall, tall ladder, Badger repaired the roof and stopped the leak.

"I fixed it," he said proudly, and laughed.

Once again they had a wonderful visit. "You must come tomorrow," said Grandmother Mouse when Badger was ready to leave.

When he returned the next day, Grandmother Mouse was waiting at the gate.

"Oh, Mr. Badger," she cried. "Thank you for fixing that sticking door, those banging shutters, and the leaky roof. Now this sweet little house is perfect, just perfect—except for . . ."

"The chimney that smokes," said Badger boldly. "It just needs sweeping!" With a special brush he made himself, Badger swept the chimney clean.

"I fixed it," he said masterfully.

Never had they laughed as much as they did that afternoon. "Please come again tomorrow," said Grandmother Mouse when it was time for Badger to leave.

But when he returned the next day there was so much noise coming from inside the house, he had to knock for a long time before Grandmother Mouse heard him.

"Oh, Mr. Badger," she cried. "Thank you for fixing this sticking door, those banging shutters, the leaky roof, and that smoking chimney. Now that everything is fixed, this dear little house really is perfect."

"Everything is fixed!" said Badger in dismay.

"Everything," said Grandmother Mouse. "Except that all my relations have come to stay, and now there's not enough room for me."

"I can fix that, too!" shouted Badger happily.

Grandmother Mouse and all her relations moved into Badger's large new house, and Badger moved back into his cozy old home.

"Now that everything is fixed, my little house is perfect," he told Grandmother Mouse the next time they met. "Except that now it needs a friend to come to tea."

"I can fix that," said Grandmother Mouse.

And she did.